Cookies

A Mr. and Mrs. Green Adventure

KEITH BAKER

sandpiper

sandpiper

HOUGHTON MIFFLIN HARCOURT
Boston   New York

For Ginger, who understands green

The text of this book is set in Giovanni Book.
The illustrations were done in acrylic paint on illustration board.

The Library of Congress has cataloged
On the Go with Mr. and Mrs. Green as follows:
Baker, Keith, 1953–
On the go with Mr. and Mrs. Green/Keith Baker.
p. cm.
"Book Four."
ISBN: 978-0-15-205762-6 hardcover
ISBN: 978-0-15-205867-8 paperback
Summary. Mr. and Mrs. Green, a loving alligator couple,
practice magic tricks, bake cookies, and dream up new inventions.
[1. Magic tricks—Fiction 2. Cookies—Fiction 3. Inventions—Fiction 4. Alligators—Fiction
5. Humorous stories.] I. Title: On the go with Mr. and Mrs. Green II. Title.
PZ7.B17427On 2006
[Fic]—dc22 2005002660

ISBN: 978-0-547-74959-4 paper over board
ISBN: 978-0-547-74561-9 paperback

Manufactured in Singapore
TWP 10 9 8 7 6 5 4 3 2 1

4500352719

Cookies

Mr. Green woke up from his nap.
He smelled cookies, *freshly baked* cookies.

He followed his nose.

(He had a big nose—it was easy to follow.)

There *were* freshly baked cookies.

And a note. It was from Mrs. Green.

Terrible?
thought Mr. Green.
DO NOT EAT?

He and Mrs. Green had baked *millions* of cookies—
none of them terrible. What was wrong with these?

Had Mrs. Green forgotten the butter?

The sugar?

The flour?

The spices?

No . . . Mr. Green could *smell* these things.

Had she forgotten the chocolate chips?

The butterscotch bits?

The peanut pieces?

The miniature marshmallow morsels?

No . . . Mr. Green could *see* these things.

What else could be wrong?

There was only one way to find out.

He took a bite.

Snappity-snap . . .

crunchity-crunch . . .

chewity-chew . . .

deeeeeeeeee-licious!

But were they *all* delicious?
Mrs. Green would want to know.

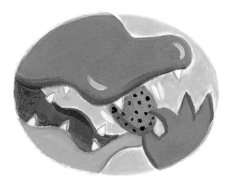

So he ate another . . .

and another . . .

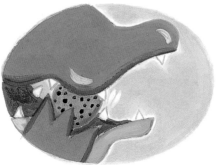

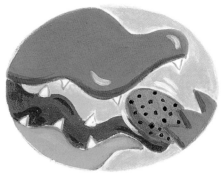

and another . . .

down to the very last cookie
(and every single crumb).

Yes—all of them were,
indeed,
deeeeeeeeee-licious!

Then the kitchen door opened.
Mrs. Green was back.

She saw the crumbs on Mr. Green's chin.

She saw his bulging belly.

She saw the empty cookie sheet.

But she didn't see any cookies anywhere.

"I ate them ALL!"
Mr. Green confessed.
"Every one had snap,
crunch, *and* chew!
Yummmm . . .
deeeeeeeeee-licious!"

"Thank you!"
said Mrs. Green.
"I knew you would like them."

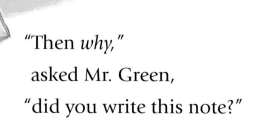

"Then *why*,"
asked Mr. Green,
"did you write this note?"

Mrs. Green took the note and opened it.
There were two pages, not one.

Mr. Green read the note again—*now* it made sense!

"You doubled the recipe?"

"Yes," said Mrs. Green, "you always ask for more,
so I used two times the ingredients—
and there are twice as many cookies."

She opened the refrigerator.
The second batch was ready to go.
"Shall we bake these now?"
she asked.

Mr. Green was not
listening—

he was calculating cookies.

"What if we double the *doubled* recipe?" he asked.

"And then double that!

And double it again!

And again! And again! And again!

And . . ."

(He ran out of breath.)

"We would need more milk . . . ," said Mrs. Green,

"and a *much* bigger cookie jar."